D1459378

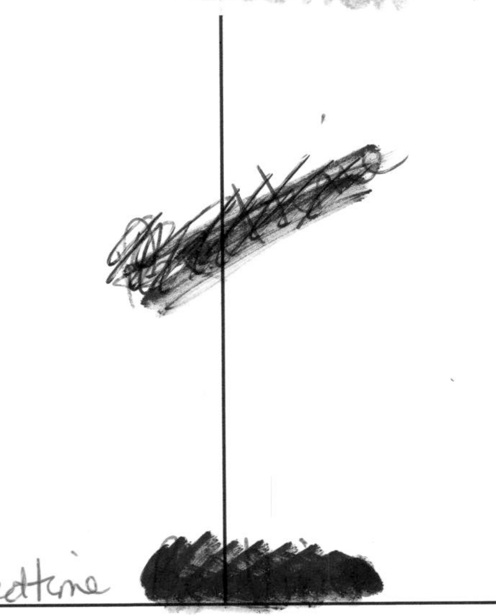

First published in the United Kingdom in 2010 by
The Chicken House, 2 Palmer Street, Frome, Somerset, BA11 1DS
www.doublecluck.com

Printed and bound in Malaysia for Imago

1 3 5 7 9 10 8 6 4 2

British Library Cataloguing in
Publication Data available
Library of Congress Cataloguing in
Publication data available

Hardback ISBN 978-1-906427-21-4
Paperback ISBN 978-1-906427-24-5

In memory of my Granda,
with love from Missy Baa
- *A.M.*

To Jasmine
- *H.S.*

Anna McQuinn
and
Hannah Shaw

The Sleep Sheep

THE CHICKEN HOUSE

Sylvie couldn't sleep.

She'd drunk her chocolate milk.

Her mother had read her three stories.

She'd asked for a glass of water – three times.

Now
she
was
bored!
TOM'S MIDNIGHT GARDEN
GOOD NIGHT MOON

'You're exasperating, Sylvie,' said her mother.
'I can't help it, Mummy,' said Sylvie.
'I'm not **trying** to be exasperating, I just can't sleep!'
'Why don't you try counting sheep?' suggested her mum.

Sylvie closed her eyes tightly
and imagined hundreds
and hundreds of sheep . . .

'I can't possibly count all of these,'
she sighed.

Then she tried to imagine them all in one long line.
'That'll be a lot easier,' she thought.

But no sooner had the sheep got in a line
than they started to dance . . .

'No, no, no!'
shouted Sylvie.
'Stand still or
I can't count you!'

But the sheep just
kept on jigging!

'Now YOU'RE exasperating!'
said Sylvie,
but at that,
the sheep took off . . .

the SLEEP SHEEP
EQUIPMENT HIRE
FOR HIRE
SKATES
BIKES
SCOOTERS
BOARDS
BOATS
SWIMWEAR
GAMES
ZZOOM!

They grabbed rollerblades and heelies, scooters and skateboards, and headed off over the hill. Sylvie had to run really fast to keep up.

'Wait!' she panted. 'How can I count you if you won't keep still?'

The sheep came to a sudden stop at a sandy beach.
Before Sylvie could catch her breath,

they were putting on

trunks and bikinis,

swimsuits and armbands.

In no time at all they were all in the water.

The ones who couldn't swim

paddled by the edge.

Finally, in twos and threes, they came out of the water. Then they sat back and relaxed.

Some played cards,

some played games on their mobile phones,

some read fairy stories,

one even did a quick spot of flower arranging.

Four set up a complex board game with rules Sylvie had never heard of,

and one elderly lady sheep had brought her knitting.

Then,
one by one,
they fell asleep . . .

'Hey, sheep,'
said Sylvie, 'now
you're REALLY
exasperating! I'm the
one who's supposed to go
to sleep, not you!'

But then she noticed -
because the sheep were still,

they were easier to count -

'one, two, three, four, five . . .'

z Z

And before she knew it,
she'd fallen asleep.

As she slept,

one by one,

the sheep got up

and tiptoed away.

If Sylvie had been awake,
she'd have heard the old one say . . .

choc milk
GOOD NIGHT MOON
A DREAM COME TRUE
TOMS MIDNIGHT GARDEN

'Whew, I'm exhausted,
I thought she'd never nod off!'